Mabel's Topsy-Turvy Homes

by Candy Wellins   illustrated by Jess Rose

beaming ☀ books
MINNEAPOLIS

For Mom and Dad,
who gave me two different adventures.
—CW

For my family.
—JR

Text copyright © 2022 Candy Wellins
Illustrations by Jess Rose, copyright © 2022 Beaming Books

Published in 2022 by Beaming Books, an imprint of 1517 Media. All rights reserved. No part of this book may be reproduced without the written permission of the publisher. Email copyright@1517.media. Printed in the United States of America.

28 27 26 25 24 23 22   1 2 3 4 5 6 7 8

Hardcover ISBN: 978-1-5064-8286-6
eBook ISBN: 978-1-5064-8287-3

Library of Congress Cataloging-in-Publication Data

Names: Wellins, Candy, author. | Rose, Jess (Jessica), illustrator.
Title: Mabel's topsy-turvy homes / by Candy Wellins ; illustrated by Jess
  Rose.
Description: Minneapolis, MN : Beaming Books, 2022. | Audience: Ages 5-8. |
  Summary: Mabel's new living situation now that her parents have split
  has her feeling topsy-turvy, but a weekend caring for the class pet
  helps her realize that having two homes is not such a bad thing after
  all.
Identifiers: LCCN 2021058119 (print) | LCCN 2021058120 (ebook) | ISBN
  9781506482866 (hardcover) | ISBN 9781506482873 (ebook)
Subjects: CYAC: Home--Fiction. | Iguanas as pets--Fiction. | LCGFT: Picture
  books.
Classification: LCC PZ7.1.W435525 Mab 2022 (print) | LCC PZ7.1.W435525
  (ebook) | DDC [E]--dc23
LC record available at https://lccn.loc.gov/2021058119
LC ebook record available at https://lccn.loc.gov/2021058120

VN0004589; 9781506482866; AUG2022

Beaming Books
PO Box 1209
Minneapolis, MN 55440-1209
Beamingbooks.com

This is Mabel.

This is Mabel's house.

And this is also Mabel's house.

Mabel doesn't like having two houses.
She finds it very confusing.

Especially when her bedroom is upstairs . . .

but also downstairs.

Jumping on the bed is never allowed . . .

but also encouraged.

The way to the bathroom is down the hall and to the left . . .

but also to the right.

Every single day, Mabel has the exact same thing for breakfast: a green smoothie and a bowl of oatmeal . . .

unless it's an egg and cheese sandwich,

a piece of peanut butter toast,
a slice of leftover pizza,

or blueberry pancakes
every other Sunday.

Her life is so topsy-turvy, it makes her want to scream!
But she can't scream. That would scare Izzy.

Izzy is the class pet iguana, and it's Mabel's turn
to care for her this weekend.

Mabel flops on her bed and flips through the adventures written in Izzy's travel journal.

Charlie took Izzy to a football game.

Delaine took her apple picking.

Emmy had Izzy the weekend of the big storm, and she and Izzy had to live without power for a whole day.

Mabel remembers that weekend
because she lost power at her house too.
But instead of living in the dark,
she went to her other house.

Charlie

Delaine

Emmy

Izzy trick-or-treated with Ben and went camping with Lulu.

She watched the new *Space Ninjas* movie at both Kaya's and Peter's houses.

Ben

Lulu ☆

Kaya

Peter

Mabel loved that movie.
She watched it at both
of her houses too.

Izzy made gingerbread with Jasmine and went skating with Ian.

Then she celebrated Hanukkah with Nora and Christmas with Keller.

Mabel likes getting to celebrate holidays twice too. It usually means twice the presents . . . and twice the hugs.

Izzy is one lucky iguana going on so many adventures.
Maybe Mabel is one lucky girl?

She can help prepare dinner by
cutting the tomatoes, stirring the sauce . . .

and tipping the delivery man.

She can enjoy warm bubble baths . . .

and hot showers.

Then she can slip into her favorite princess nightgown . . .
and her favorite superhero pjs.

Every single night, it's (not) the exact same thing: snuggling on the couch and reading a story . . .

unless she's giggling and
avoiding the tickle monster.

Two houses means two bedrooms to decorate.
Two houses means occasional breaks from oatmeal . . .
and occasional breaks from takeout.
And two houses means double the fun.

This is Mabel.

This is Mabel's adventure.

And these are Mabel's homes.

About the Author and Illustrator

CANDY WELLINS is a former elementary school teacher and has a BA in journalism and a master's in literacy education. She's now a full-time mom to three wonderful children who keep her up-to-date and immersed in children's literature. She is the author of *Saturdays Are for Stella* and *The Stars Beckoned: Edward White's Amazing Walk in Space*. She and her family make their home in Central Texas.

JESS ROSE is an illustrator and designer living in Yorkshire, England. She has loved to draw her entire life, creating characters and helping tell stories that children can relate to. She has two children and uses her experience as a parent to inspire her work.